Just what kind of monkey business
has befallen Mr. Hound's shop?
Who has broken his window?
And most importantly: why?

Luckily, our team of plucky detectives has been chomping at the bit to take on their first case. When Mr. Hound hires them to investigate, they hoof it to his shop. And once they get sleuthing, wild horses couldn't drag them away from the scent of a clue. But is it all just a dog and pony show to distract them from the truth?

Idioms are everywhere in the Gumshoe Zoo detective agency's hilarious first case as they attempt to get to the bottom of Mr. Hound's mystery.

"This enjoyable introduction to idiomatic speech gives lots of laughs, a mystery to solve, and a funny cliff-hanger."
—*School Library Journal*

"Good-humored and stimulating. Really, it's the bee's knees."
—*Kirkus Reviews*

"A highly entertaining comic mystery."
—*Publishers Weekly*

"Give this to a kid who enjoys puzzles and witty turns of phrase." —Shelf Awareness

A Parents' Choice Recommended Seal

Amina's

ENTER

To my buddy Greyson: You're the bee's knees.

First Chronicle Books LLC paperback edition, published in 2017.
Originally published in hardcover in 2015 by Chronicle Books LLC.

ISBN 978-1-4521-6435-9

The Library of Congress has cataloged the original edition as follows:

Nichols, Travis, author.
Fowl play / by Travis Nichols.
pages cm.
Summary: A team of animal sleuths is hired to solve the mystery of a broken window.
ISBN 978-1-4521-3182-5 (alk. paper)
1. Animals—Juvenile fiction. 2. Humorous stories. [1. Mystery and detective stories. 2. English language—Idioms—Fiction. 3. Animals—Fiction. 4. Humorous stories.] I. Title.
PZ7.N544Fo 2015
[E]—dc23

2014024307

Manufactured in China.

Design by Ryan Hayes.
Lettering by Travis Nichols.
The illustrations in this book were rendered in pencil on paper and colored digitally.

10 9 8 7 6 5 4 3 2 1

Chronicle Books LLC
680 Second Street
San Francisco, California 94107

FOWL
PLAY
A Mystery Told
in Idioms!
by Travis Nichols
chronicle books · san francisco
Looks like another dull as dishwater day.
ALERT

ALERT

GUMSHOE ZOO!
In a pickle?

Hello, detective agency? This is Mr. Hound.
GUMSHOE ZOO
DETECTIVE AGENCY
63-6802

GUMSHOE ZOO
DETECTIVE AGENCY

I need your help.

Mike
You've got your goat, sir. We're on the case!
Josie
BEEP
BEEP
ALERT
Sharon
Antoine

eggie
All right, team. Opportunity knocks!
Steve
Morgan
Four... five... six...
Quentin
GUMSHOE ZOO

Thanks for coming, detectives. Someone broke my store window last night.

We'll take it from here, Mr. Hound.

Hmm... Yes. There's something fishy going on around here.

Oh! No offense, Reggie.
None taken.

But you are right.

window:
-glass
-broken

There is some definite monkey business at hand, my friend.

Ooh. I didn't mean anything by that, Steve.
No sweat.
ENTER

And I agree. I smell a rat.

Yikes! Sorry, Josie.
I understand.

I, too, suspect foul play.

Oh! Morgan! I apologize.
No need, Josie. That was F-O-U-L. I'm a chicken. That's F-O-W-L.

Now let's grab the bull by the horns and solve this case!

Hey!

Sorry about that. I just thought...

It's cool. Water off a duck's back.

Oops! Sharon. I am SO sorry.
Don't mention it, buddy.

Hold it.

I don't think I'm barking up the wrong tree here. Whoops... sorry, Mr. Hound.

Sure sure sure. Um... hey... I think there's some... um... evidence... away from here.

Look! A mistake in the lettering!

So what?

So maybe you saw the mistake on your window, but you didn't want to pay an arm and a leg to fix it.

Mr. Hound's
Grociries
open 7-7 M-F

So you cooked up a scheme to break it . . .

. . . and called us so you could get it fixed for free.

A-HA! That's IT, isn't it?

What's the matter? Cat got your tongue?

Hold your horses! I won't be your scapegoat!

HOW DARE YOU!

You're all canned! Beat it!

No, YOU'RE the one who's canned.
You're under arrest.

It's time to face the music.

You gotta reap what you sow.

It's the price you have to pay.

The chickens have come home to roost.

Sorry, Morgan.

It's fine. Let's just wrap this up.

Take him to the big house, officers.
Way to use your noodle, Sharon!

This is W-IDM reporting live at the scene of a crime just solved by a group of brilliant detectives.

Yes, the sky's the limit for—what's that?

We interrupt this story to bring you an urgent report of a situation developing downtown.
W-IDM 4

Get those detectives over here. On the double.
It's a... jumbo... shrimp.
MAYOR

The idiom-tastic case of the broken window was a breeze, but will our favorite sleuths be able to solve the mystery behind this beast of oxymoronic proportions?

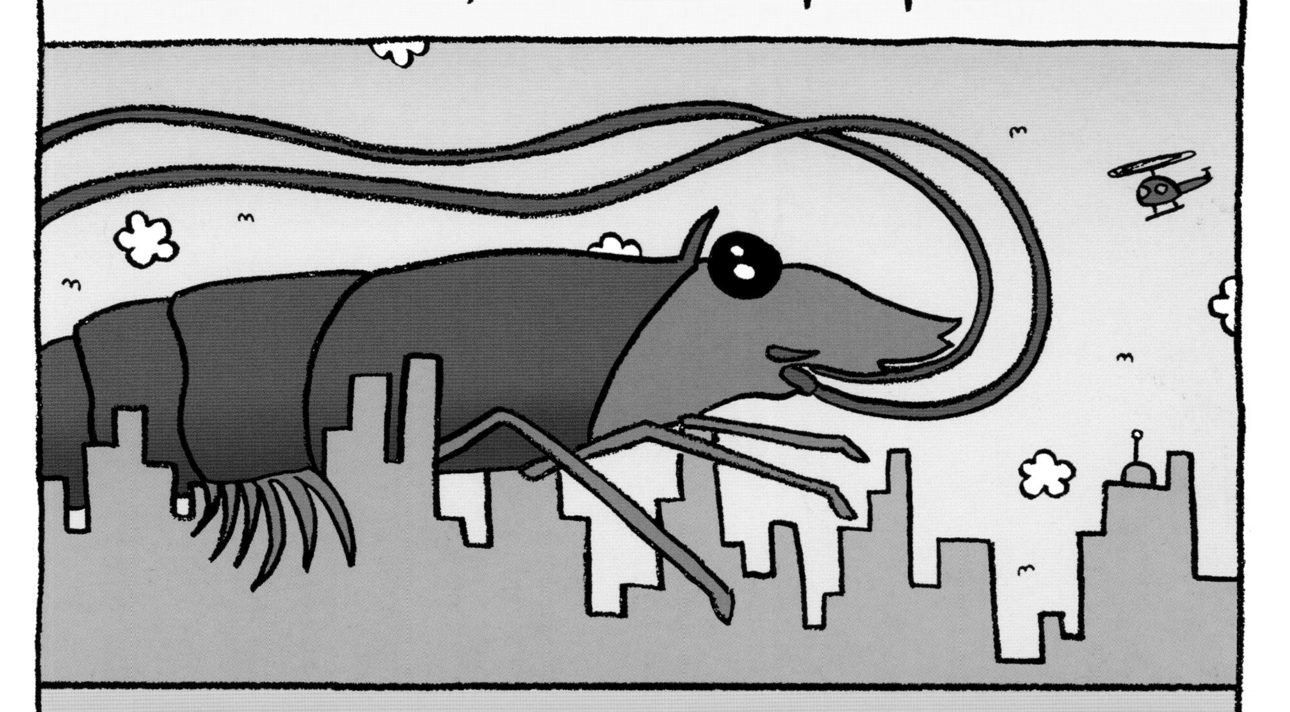

STAY TUNED!

An idiom is a group of words that means something other than the literal meaning. For example, "to rain cats and dogs" doesn't mean that it's actually raining cats and dogs. Rather, it means that it's raining super hard.

Some idioms have meanings that are understandable by context ("You've got gossip about Nate? I'm all ears!"), and some have origins in stories and history (to "cry wolf" comes from one of Aesop's fables).

There are idioms in all languages. In fact, it's estimated that there are around 25,000 in the English language alone! Here are the idioms found in this book.

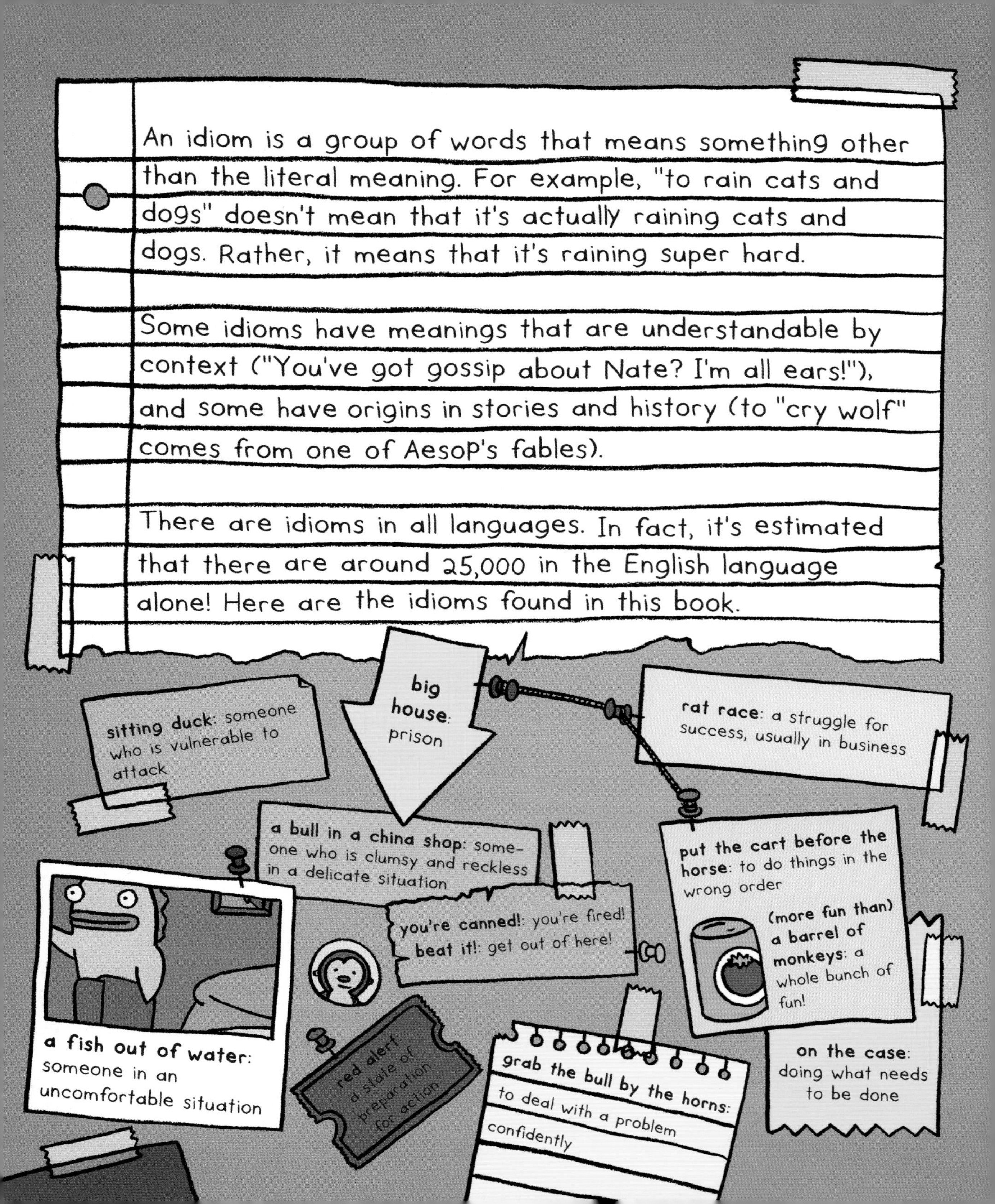

face the music: to accept the punishment you deserve
on the double: quickly, now!
in a pickle: a difficult situation
water off a duck's back: something that has no effect
reap what you sow: accept the consequences of your actions
the price you have to pay: see above
wrap it up: to stop what you're doing, to finish what you started
use your noodle: to think, to figure it out
dull as dishwater: extremely boring
barking up the wrong tree: making the wrong choice, the wrong assumption
pay an arm and a leg: to pay a lot of money
cook up: to plan, to scheme
cat got your tongue?: why aren't you talking?
hold your horses: wait, slow down
scapegoat: someone wrongly blamed
the chickens have come home to roost: something bad or foolish from the past has returned and is going to cause problems
ELITE TAXI SE
508-8
something fishy (or "smells fishy"): something suspicious
monkey business: silliness, trickiness, or dishonesty
smell a rat: to suspect something is wrong
foul play: something illegal, dishonest, or unfair
no sweat: don't worry, no problem
don't count your chickens before they hatch: wait until what you're expecting to happen actually happens before moving forward
the sky's the limit: anything is possible!
a breeze: something easy
get your goat: usually means to annoy you, but Quentin uses it literally
k
stay tuned: we'll be back!

Amina's

FUTURE HQ
of
GUMSHOE ZOO
ENTER

Travis Nichols writes and illustrates books and comics for kids and post-kids, including the companion to this book, *Betty's Burgled Bakery: An Alliteration Adventure*. His love of words and language comes from his family of teachers and lawyers and teachers and writers (and also teachers). Mysteries solved include "The Case of the Dropped Contact Lens" and "What's for Lunch?" He's a Texpatriate now living in San Francisco. You can find out more at www.iamtravisnichols.com.